For my library friends,
Best wishes,

Jeanne Moran

MIKEY AND THE SWAMP MONSTER

By Jeanne Moran

Illustrated by
Michael Rausch

JM: For Mikeys everywhere

MR: To my dad. For signing me up for art classes
when he realized I was bad at soccer.

jeannemoran.weebly.com   michaeljprausch.com

We've got company, Mikey.

I'll be right down, Mom!

Mikey knew what that meant.
The Swamp Monster was back.

Last time the Swamp Monster came to Mikey's house, it slithered
EVERYWHERE.

It slimed the rug and slobbered the furniture.

WAAOooo?

That Swamp Monster crashed Mikey's favorite block tower.

It screamed and **HOOOWLED**

worse than his neighbor's dog.

Plus, the Swamp Monster smelled bad —
worse than a garbage can

and worse than a skunk.

It smelled worse than a garbage dumpster full of skunks.

When the Swamp Monster left,
Mikey's whole house stank.

That beast wouldn't come in Mikey's house again.
Mikey would stop him.

Mikey packed his monster-stopper kit,

and climbed to the top of a tree for a better look.

The Swamp Monster was near Mikey's front door! And it was holding his Aunt Fay!

Mikey had to help.

Mikey crept
    to the top of a cliff
        and listened...

OH, NO!
The Swamp Monster was already in his house!

Mikey gripped the monster-catcher with his teeth.

He crept closer...

...and closer
AND CLOSER...

... until he was close enough to smell the terrible beast.

I'll SAVE YOU

THE END ?

Made in the USA
Middletown, DE
06 September 2016